A Note to Parents

Read to your child...

★ Reading aloud is one of the best ways to develop your child's love of reading. Read together at least 20 minutes each day.

★ Laughter is contagious! Read with feeling. Show your child that reading is fun.

★ Take time to answer questions your child may have about the story. Linger over pages that interest your child.

...and your child will read to you.

★ Follow cues from your child to know when he wants to join in the reading.

★ Support your young reader. Give him a word whenever he asks for it.

★ Praise your child as he progresses. Your encouraging words will build his confidence.

You can help your Level 1 reader.

★ Reading begins with knowing how a book works. Show your child the title and where the story begins.

★ Ask your child to find picture clues on each page. Talk about what is happening in the story.

★ Point to the words as you read so your child can make the connection between the print and the story.

★ Ask your child to point to words she knows.

★ Let your child supply the rhyming words.

Most of all, enjoy your reading time together!

> **—Bernice Cullinan, Ph.D.,**
> **Professor of Reading, New York University**

Reader's Digest Children's Books
Reader's Digest Road, Pleasantville, NY 10570-7000
Copyright © 1999 Reader's Digest Children's Publishing, Inc.
All rights reserved. Reader's Digest Children's Books and All-Star Readers are
trademarks and Reader's Digest is a registered trademark
of The Reader's Digest Association, Inc.
Fisher-Price trademarks are used under license from
Fisher-Price, Inc., a subsidiary of Mattel, Inc., East Aurora, NY 14052.
Printed in Hong Kong.
10 9 8 7 6 5 4 3 2 1

Library of Congress Cataloging-in-Publication Data

Hood, Susan.
    Oops! I made a mistake / by Susan Hood ; illustrated by Dana Regan.
    p. cm. — (All-star readers. Level 1)
    Summary: A little girl learns that everyone makes mistakes sometimes.
    ISBN 1-57584-295-5 (pbk. : alk. paper)
    [1. Behavior—Fiction. 2. Stories in rhyme.]
    I. Regan, Dana, ill. II. Title. III. Series.
PZ8.3.H7577 Oo   1999   [E]—dc21   98-49566

Oops!
I Made a Mistake

by Susan Hood
illustrated by Dana Regan

All-Star Readers™

Reader's Digest Children's Books™

Pleasantville, New York • Montréal, Québec

I skip in the door.

6

I made a mistake.

Oops!

I made a mistake.

The puppy got out.

A big, BIG mistake!

My dad drops his rake.

But he does not shout.

"It was just a mistake.

There's no need to pout."

We bring back our cat.

We bring back our pup.

We put things away

and help Dad clean up.

We all make mistakes.

Even Ben.

Even Brad.

We all make mistakes.

Even my dad!

Color in the star next to each word you can read.

☆ a   ☆ got   ☆ out

☆ all   ☆ he   ☆ paint

☆ and   ☆ help   ☆ pout

☆ away   ☆ his   ☆ pup

☆ back   ☆ I   ☆ puppy

☆ Ben   ☆ in   ☆ put

☆ big   ☆ it   ☆ rake

☆ Brad   ☆ just   ☆ shout

☆ bring   ☆ made   ☆ skip

☆ but   ☆ make   ☆ the

☆ cat   ☆ mistake   ☆ there's

☆ clean   ☆ my   ☆ things

☆ dad   ☆ need   ☆ to

☆ does   ☆ no   ☆ up

☆ door   ☆ not   ☆ was

☆ drops   ☆ on   ☆ we

☆ even   ☆ oops

☆ floor   ☆ our